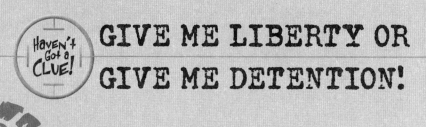

GIVE ME LIBERTY OR
GIVE ME DETENTION!

BY KENNY ABDO

ILLUSTRATED BY BOB DOUCET

visit us at www.abdopublishing.com

Published by Magic Wagon, a division of the ABDO Group,
PO Box 398166, Minneapolis, Minnesota 55439. Copyright © 2014
by Abdo Consulting Group, Inc. International copyrights reserved in all
countries. All rights reserved. No part of this book may be reproduced
in any form without written permission from the publisher.

Calico Chapter Books™ is a trademark and logo of Magic Wagon.

Printed in the United States of America, North Mankato, Minnesota.
062013
092013

Text by Kenny Abdo
Illustrations by Bob Doucet
Edited by Karen Latchana Kenney
Cover and interior design by Colleen Dolphin, Mighty Media, Inc.

Library of Congress Cataloging-in-Publication Data
Abdo, Kenny, 1986-
  Give me liberty or give me detention! / Kenny Abdo ; illustrated by
Bob Doucet.
      p. cm. – (Haven't got a clue!)
  Summary: When his project blows up and ruins the science fair, Henry
Gallagher asks fourth-grade detective Jon Gummyshoes to investigate
an obvious case of sabotage, but this mystery is complicated by school
politics.
  ISBN 978-1-61641-953-0
1. Science projects–Juvenile fiction. 2. Science fairs–Juvenile fiction.
3. Sabotage–Juvenile fiction. 4. Elementary schools–Juvenile fiction.
[1. Mystery and detective stories. 2. Science projects–Fiction.
3. Science fairs–Fiction. 4. Sabotage–Fiction. 5. Elementary schools–
Fiction. 6. Schools–Fiction.] I. Doucet, Bob, ill. II. Title.
  PZ7.A1589334Giv 2013
  813.6–dc23
                              2013001068

Table of Contents

The Usual Suspects 4

Note from the Detective's Files 6

CHAPTER 1: From the Beginning 8

CHAPTER 2: A Bit of a Bust 16

CHAPTER 3: The Tough Spot 22

CHAPTER 4: Looney Tunes Business 27

CHAPTER 5: Mr. Cragg 37

CHAPTER 6: Stolen Solution 46

CHAPTER 7: Desperate Words 51

CHAPTER 8: Word for Word 57

CHAPTER 9: The Combination 66

CHAPTER 10: The Hard Answers 73

A Page from Gummyshoes's Notebook 80

The Usual Suspects
THE WHO'S WHO OF THE CASE

JON
GUMMYSHOES

LAWRENCE
"LARRY"
MACGUFFIN

PRINCIPAL
LINKS

JEFF
DAWKINS

HENRY
"HANK"
GALLAGHER

DANIEL
CRAGG

Note from the Detective's Files

The name is Gummyshoes—Jon Gummyshoes.
I know what you're thinking: funny name, right?
Well, that's not what I'm here to talk about. I'm
here to tell you the facts. The cold, hard facts
about the cases I come across day in and day out
at Edwin West Elementary School.

The way I see it, trouble seems to find me
around every corner. So I make it my business to
clean it up. I don't need this game. It needs me.

The case I'm about to share with you wasn't
my first, and it certainly won't be my last. This
investigation led me into a sticky situation. The
clues were hard to find and some led to dead
ends. I wasn't sure if I could solve this case. But
in the end, the truth always explodes right in your
face. And in this case, that was definitely true.

CHAPTER 1
From the Beginning

I sat forward in my chair suddenly. I needed to get a better look at the crumpled white paper I was holding in my hands. It read:

> Henry Gallagher, fourth-grade student of Edwin West Elementary, has hereby been disqualified from this year's science fair.

I sat back in my chair and looked over the sentence a few more times. I mouthed the words as I read each one over and over again. It looked like I was singing a tune that no one wanted to hear.

He is no longer allowed to participate in any school competitions or functions due to improper behavior.

I pushed the bluc plastic chair back as far as the wall would let me. Then I stood up with the paper just inches from my eyes. I walked to the whiteboard, picked up a green marker, and flipped it a few times in the air. I continued reading the note the entire time.

Henry Gallagher shall have this incident placed in his permanent record. Principal Links will decide appropriate punishment within the week.

The room was quiet. All I could hear was the *tick-tick-ticking* of the clock to my right. I had been given permission by Principal Links to use the computer classroom as an office. You see, I had been taking on so many cases in the past couple weeks, I couldn't possibly take any more house calls. My mom just couldn't make enough fruit punch and chocolate chip bars for all the clients who needed my help. Plus, the new guests made my dog, Little Ricky, go absolutely bananas.

The room wasn't half bad. There were four rows of computers. The hum of each computer went along with the tick of the clock like some strange, electronic orchestra.

I gave the marker one more flip, then placed it back on the whiteboard ledge. Without taking my eyes off of the paper, I made my way back to the blue plastic chair. I parked myself in it and scooted it back up to the table.

The sun was still out, pushing itself through the window behind my head. It illuminated the words written in pencil on that crumpled piece of paper.

... has hereby been disqualified from this year's science fair.

Then a loud sigh forced me to lower the crumpled piece of white paper. I stared at the boy who sat in the seat next to me.

"I don't know what to tell ya', Henry," I said. "These seem like some serious roasted potatoes that have been thrown your way."

Henry squirmed a little in his chair and then straightened. Henry was about my height, maybe a little taller. He had greasy, brown-blond hair that he tried to make nice by slicking back. Some of it draped over his forehead, not doing him any good.

"Gee, Jon. I don't know what to do," he whined, twisting a baseball cap in his fists. "I'm in real trouble here. I need your help."

I sat back in the chair again and sighed. Then I put my hands in both pockets and searched. Finally I pulled out a half-pack of gum and dug a stick out for myself. I offered a stick to Henry.

A smile formed on Henry's face and the grip on his hat loosened.

"Aw, no thanks. I gave that stuff up a while ago," he said. "You know, on account of the cavities and all. I'm on a first-name basis with my dentist now."

"Probably a good call there, Hank. Your teeth will last a lot longer without this." I waited a few seconds. "Do you mind if I call you Hank?"

He loosened up a bit more. "Gee, my own mother calls me Jason sometimes. She doesn't even know anyone named Jason! Well," he snorted, "except for me. I guess I'm just a face that you can't remember." He frowned. "To be honest, I think that's why I could never run for any type of student council position. You won't be voting for a mug that no one recognizes."

I shoved the gum into my mouth and gave it a few good chews. Then I tapped my right index finger on top of the note Hank had handed to me.

"Never mind that," I said, lifting the paper off of the desk again. "You wrote this?"

"Sure did," Hank replied twisting up his cap again.

"Principal Links was there? He saw you?" I asked.

"Yep. He stood over my shoulder the entire time I was writing it out. He even told me all of the words I had to scratch." He looked down at his mangled baseball hat and then back up at me. "You gotta help me, Gummyshoes. I didn't do it, honest! It's all a big setup, I swear."

"And you have to have this signed by your mom before Principal Links can put ya behind the eight ball?" I asked.

"That's the idea, which puts me in a pickle all on its own," he said.

"How do you figure?" I asked, raising an eyebrow.

"Well, the thing is, my folks are on a trip right now," he said. "I'm being taken care of by my grandpaps."

"Okay, great," I said, sitting up. "That should give us some time then."

"Time for what?" Hank shakily asked. "Jon, until I get this paper signed, I'm going to be in detention every day after school."

"Well, then you take the time in detention as long as you can, ya hear?" I sternly instructed. "I'll figure this out for you. That's a promise, Hank."

His nervous face turned into a confused one. "And how can you make that promise, Jon?"

I sat forward in the chair and placed my hands together. "Some kids win the science fair. Others, they go to state playing soccer." I pulled my hands apart and placed them flat on the desk. "Me? I solve mysteries." I sat back in my chair and got comfortable. "Now, let's hear it from the beginning."

CHAPTER 2

A Bit of a Bust

Hank laid it all out for me as I took notes about the case. I hadn't been around when the science fair was going on. I was in the middle of a pretty heavy case at the time with my best pal and partner, Larry MacGuffin.

The science fair was in the school gymnasium. Rows of tables were filled with great entries. Frankie Flats, Edwin West's resident goofball, spent two months with a nest of cockroaches for his project. Becky Lipgloss tried watering daisy seeds with anything but water. Instead she used orange juice, energy drinks, you name it. I wasn't there to see the results, but I can just tell you that it didn't work.

I saw Amber Holiday's project before she brought it to the gymnasium. It was actually a swell idea. She noticed that the stomach of an ant turned white when it drank milk. So she had three ants drink three different types of food coloring. Each of their stomachs turned the shade of the food coloring it drank. It was strange, but really cool, to see multi-colored ants.

But back to the case. As Hank was telling me, he wasn't looking for a medal or ribbon for his project. And from how he described the display, it sounded like he wasn't joking. He mixed six cups of flour, two cups of salt, four tablespoons of cooking oil, and two cups of water. He molded the sticky mixture around a jar to make a volcano. It didn't look like a volcano, though. It looked like a deformed cake.

Just before he had to present his project, Hank put on his plastic gloves and mixed his volcano solution together. He put baking soda, dish soap, and some red food coloring in a jar. He was good to go for the eruption. Then the tricky part came in. Hank took off his gloves, placed them next to the volcano, and walked to the water fountain to get a drink.

By the time he was back at his display, Principal Links was just one project away. Hank reached for his gloves, only they weren't where he had left them. They were on the ground, which seemed strange. But he reached down, picked them up, and put them on.

"And here we have, let's see...," Principal Links said, making his way up to Hank's project, "Stephen Goldner."

"It's actually Henry Gallagher, sir," Hank corrected sheepishly.

"Oh, I see," Links replied, flipping through his clipboard. "You must be the new student."

"I've actually been here since kindergarten, sir," he told Links.

"Right," Links said, lowering his clipboard. "Well, what do you have to show us?" Links examined the volcano. "This is a mighty impressive diagram of a *Tyrannosaurus rex* here, Henry."

"Actually, sir, this is a functioning model of a volcano," Hank said. "Here is the vinegar needed to form a reaction. The reaction will cause an eruption of lava from the volcano. Once I've mixed this vinegar with what's in the jar, carbon dioxide gas will be created. The gas will force the lava out of the volcano." He started to pour the vinegar in and said, "Like so."

But there was something wrong with the reaction. It made Hank stop in his tracks. His model began to shake and pieces of the volcano began falling off.

"Henry, what is going on here?" Links asked nervously.

"I don't know, sir. I did everything I was supposed to," Hank said, pushing his gloves into the volcano to keep it from bursting. But the gloves only made it worse.

"Everybody, run! It's going to blow!" Frankie screamed as the volcano shook on top of the table.

And just as Frankie screamed, the volcano exploded. It sprayed red foam. Parts of the sticky volcano flew around the giant gym. It hit everyone and their projects. Diagrams of DNA were drenched. Models of cities and tsunamis were ripped apart and thrown every which way. All in all, the Edwin West science fair was a bit of a bust.

The last thing Hank remembered was lying flat on the gym floor in a puddle of lava and papers from Principal Links's clipboard. He heard the panic and chaos throughout the gym. He lifted his head slightly and saw the green, red, and orange ants from Amber's project scurrying to safety. Then he passed out.

CHAPTER 3
The Tough Spot

I sat back in the blue plastic chair and stared into Hank's eyes.

"So that's that?" I asked, rubbing my chin thoughtfully.

"That's that?" Hank repeated eyes wide open. "The gymnasium was destroyed, Jon—by my science fair project!"

I stood up, saying, "Ah, quit bumping your gums, Hank. I told you, I'll handle this. Everything will be fine."

I walked over to the coatrack. I handed Hank his coat and then put on my own.

Hank pulled his coat on and zipped it up. "And how, might I ask, are you going to handle this?"

We stepped out of the computer room and I closed the door behind me. We walked toward the exit of the school. I got to the door, pushed it open, and let Hank out first. The sun had just gone down and it was cold. The sky was purple with swirls of orange and red. The snow was doing a dance around the glow of the lamppost. I rubbed my hands together to get warm.

"Listen, Hank, I have your story. I just need to find a few missing pieces tomorrow. I've done this kind of thing before. And I always find the answers." I patted Hank on the back.

Hank frowned and said, "Yeah, well, I'll be in detention every day after school until this is figured out. I'm counting on you."

I let out a small laugh and began walking home. "Get some rest, Hank," I said with my back to him.

The snow was slowly falling. I made footprints on the white sidewalk, listening to the crack of fresh snow beneath my winter boots. I had left my mittens at home, or maybe I lost them. Either way, I did my best to keep my hands warm in my coat pockets. All I thought about was the note Hank had been forced to write to his parents, confessing to a crime he didn't commit. Now it was my problem to fix. And I didn't even know the kid. We were classmates, but I had never spoken with Hank before that day.

I slid a stick of gum out of my coat pocket, unwrapped it, and found it a home in my mouth. I thought about the case while I chewed. I don't know what it is, but the flavor of a fresh piece of gum really gets my noggin going. Hank's science experiment went haywire even though he did everything exactly as he was supposed to. Someone had to have switched out the vinegar during the minute he was away from the table. The gloves were a giveaway, but that's far too easy.

I kept a steady pace as I walked down the street. Ice Man's Ice Cream Parlor, my usual haunt, was looking a lot more festive than usual. Paper candy canes and blinking lights framed the front window. I peered through the frosted

glass and saw many of my classmates enjoying an after-school snack. Everyone was there.

Frankie Flats was eating a banana fudge sundae the size of his body. It seemed like he had missed his mouth and introduced most of it to his T-shirt, though. James Weisenborne (formerly known as Jimmy Blues) was sipping on a root beer, talking loudly with Frankie and slapping him on the back. Larry MacGuffin, my best pal and partner, was seated next to the girl of his dreams, Becky Lipgloss. They had gotten a lot closer since they starred in the school's Thanksgiving play together. Everyone looked like they were having a great time.

Outside, I rubbed my hands together, blew sort of warm air into them, and moved on. I reached my house and stood on the walkway. *First thing tomorrow*, I thought, *I'll get going on solving this mystery.*

CHAPTER 4
Looney Tunes Business

Mornings are never fun in the middle of winter. Without my socks on, the hardwood floors were freezing. I dashed across my room to throw on my brown corduroy pants, a long undershirt, a button-down shirt, and a pair of thick socks. I made my way downstairs where my mom, Joan Gummyshoes, had laid out a great breakfast. It was scrambled eggs wrapped in a tortilla and a tall glass of orange juice. I'm told that breakfast is the most important meal of the day.

I finished my burrito in a few bites and drained the whole glass of juice without taking a breath. I sat back in the kitchen chair, patted my belly, and threw a few rogue pieces of egg down to my dog, Little Ricky.

"Jon, don't feed Little Ricky your scraps. You know he's had problems with eating things around the house. This only encourages him," my mom said as she took my plate and placed it in the sink.

"Sorry, Ma. I'm not thinking too straight today. Just a lot on my mind, I guess." I flipped through the pages of my new *Max Hamilton* comic without reading them.

"Don't forget that Uncle Nicky wants to chat with you before school tomorrow," she said.

My Uncle Nicky is from California. He is the greatest detective in the whole universe. He's my true inspiration for being a detective. Maybe he could help me with this case.

"I wouldn't miss it for the world," I said, putting my backpack on over my coat and walking out of the door.

It's amazing I could even move. The cold air felt like it was freezing all of the muscles and bones in my body. Fortunately, I could see the trusty bus driving down the street, right on time. Well, I saw it driving, but I didn't see it slowing down. I watched as the bus slid past my house, and then I started to walk toward school. I was nearly frozen by the time I reached the front doors.

Most mornings, I dreaded walking into Edwin West Elementary. That morning was no different. Word had spread that Henry Gallagher was the punk who destroyed the gym with his volcano. I made my way through a sea of whispers, hoping that I could just get to my locker.

"Jon, have you heard about this gym catastrophe?! Links is going to come down on Henry so hard!" I heard a familiar voice say. I turned and put my hand over his mouth.

"Shh! Are you crazy?!" I whispered to MacGuffin. "Listen, this scandal is a whole lot of nonsense. Someone else detonated that volcano. They wanted to frame Hank. I'm going to find out who it was. But until then, I want it to be kept on the down-low, do you know what I mean?"

"Sure, Jon, on the down-low. No problem,"

MacGuffin responded as we approached my locker. "It's just that Becky told me that Hank did it."

I stopped spinning my combination on my lock. "Is that a fact?" I looked over at MacGuffin. "And who did Becky hear this from?"

MacGuffin stared at me for a second. "Well, I think she heard it from Frankie who heard it from James. I think he was told by the third grader who was hit by a flying chunk of volcano during the science fair."

"That little weasel," I said, clenching my fist.

MacGuffin didn't say anything, but his sigh told me all I needed to know.

"What?" I asked through my teeth.

"I guess you haven't seen the morning announcements yet," MacGuffin added.

"No, I just got to school, how would I have...," I turned around to see the TV on the hallway wall.

Jeff Dawkins was sitting behind a desk wearing a suit and tie. He was reading from a piece of paper. Below him, words on the screen read: *Scandal of the Century*. And what was the picture on the screen? It was Hank's mug.

"Breaking news in what is being called the be all and end all case in the history of Edwin West," Jeff said into the camera. "Daniel Cragg, fourth grade lawyer from Edwin East Elementary, has been asked to step in tomorrow morning to help with the punishment hearing for Henry Gallagher.

"Cragg is known for either helping teachers get to the bottom of tough cases or getting kids out of trouble. I have a feeling that Gallagher is knee-deep in a whole lot of lava," Jeff said. Then he put the paper down on the desk and said, "And now sports!"

"Jon, I just heard about your new case—the one with Henry Gallagher," Ben Christopher said from behind me. Ben was the fourth grade student council ambassador. He was up for reelection next semester. I had helped him out on a case a while back. He helped me out when I needed it.

"If there is anything I can do, please don't be afraid to ask," he said, putting his hand on my shoulder.

"I'm honestly not worried about this," I said

SCANDAL OF THE CENTU

with a slight laugh. "This is something I am completely capable of handling. I do appreciate the offer, though. I think you should be focusing on the campaign more than this kooky nonsense."

"So far the polls are all pointing at me to win. With the Thanksgiving play last week breaking ticket records, Principal Links has said he would personally endorse my reelection. He said he'd make sure I stay in office until middle school!" He smiled and then shook his head. "It really is a shame about Henry, though."

"You know him?" I asked, turning back to my locker.

"Sure do. He runs against me every election," Ben said. "His numbers are rock bottom, though. I don't ever see him as a threat to staying in office."

"Gee, that's swell, Ben," I responded.

He took his hand off of my shoulder and shook my hand. "Well, just know I'm here for you if you need anything."

I nodded and Ben walked off. I took out my notebook and jotted down a few things. I didn't know that Hank ran in the council elections. Then I turned around and started walking. Within a few seconds I was through Links's office door and slamming it behind me.

"This is nuts, Chief. Pure, 100 percent looney tunes business," I said, pacing in front of his desk.

"I don't remember saying, 'come on in,' Gummyshoes." Principal Links sighed from behind his desk.

"You have to do something! I won't be able to help Hank get off of these charges. Not with how the cards are stacked up against me...," I said. "Expel me. Give me the boot, Chief. It's the only way I can get out of this mess unharmed."

Principal Links laughed. "Gummyshoes, I'm not going to expel you just because you think you can't solve a case."

"Have you seen the evidence?!" I asked. "They have so much against him! I can't fight this battle alone, Chief. Now Daniel Cragg is coming into the picture, I don't know what I'm going to do!"

"All right, Gummyshoes, relax," Links told me.

I stopped pacing. "Well, can't you do

something? I mean, can't you expel everyone else?"

"I can't do anything," Links said. "I read the summons and it looks like the court will be held at Edwin East."

"So, talk to Principal Ant!" I said. "You guys used to be chums. Ask him for a favor!"

"I did. I brought Daniel Cragg into this," Links told me.

"Yeah, I wanted to ask you about him. How come you're leaving it up to him? Is he a real lawyer?" I asked.

"No, Gummyshoes." Links said. "Daniel is the president of the debate club. He and Principal Ant have worked on many cases together. Most of the time, Daniel pokes holes into fake statements made by accused kids. That's all."

"Can you just hold off on the punishment hearing?" I asked. "If I had more time, I might be able to crack this case!"

"No can do, Gummyshoes," Links said.

I found the seat in front of Principal Links's desk and parked myself in it. "Okay, fine. I'll build a case that will prove Hank is innocent."

"That's the spirit, Gummyshoes!" Links said. "Here's a suggestion. Go find Daniel."

I looked at Principal Links and said, "Sure, talk to Cragg. That makes sense. Thanks, Chief."

CHAPTER 5

Mr. Cragg

At noon, the lunch bell rang. I decided to skip lunch and walk over to Edwin East. I was looking for Cragg, whom I'd never met before. I figured I'd just ask around until someone gave him up. I didn't know why I was so worried. He was just a kid. He put his snow pants on one leg at a time, just like the rest of us.

It was around 12:15 p.m. when I arrived on Edwin East's campus. Lunch was still going on inside, but there were plenty of kids out on the jungle gym for recess. So I asked a few questions and wrote down a few notes.

My first mark was a younger kid climbing along the monkey bars. "Say, have you heard of Daniel Cragg?"

"Never heard of him," the kid said, swinging to the next bar.

I made my way around the jungle gym. No one there had heard of Cragg, either. I stopped next to the swings and rested against the pole. I pulled a stick of gum out of my coat, unwrapped it, and shoved it in my mouth. Soon a shorter student approached me. He was decked out in a snowsuit, gloves, and boots. His face was hidden behind a ski mask. He stopped a few feet away and stared at me.

"Anything I can help you with, kid?" I asked through chews.

"You're looking for Cragg?" the kid asked.

"Maybe I am. What's it to ya?" I asked, looking for a trash can to toss my now flavorless gum.

"The name is Phil—Phil Grant. I can take you to Cragg," he said.

"Is that so?" I said, putting the gum back in its wrapper and then the wrapper into my pocket. "You work for Cragg, then?"

"Occasionally," Phil said. "I do some small work here and there—for a price."

"Oh yeah? So what's next?" I asked the kid.

"I'll take you to him," he told me. "That's what you want, isn't it?"

I looked around. "Sure, take me to him."

We walked through the jungle gym, passing all of the third graders enjoying their recess. The mood changed once we were inside. The sun was replaced with dim fluorescent lights. We took the stairs all the way down to the bottom floor of Edwin East and hung a left. Halfway down a long hall, Phil stopped and looked at me. "Just wait out here for a second," he said.

"I'm not goin' anywhere," I replied, shoving my hands into my pockets.

He kept his eyes on me as he opened the door and disappeared through it. I waited in the hallway for what felt like a couple of minutes. Then I heard some muffled talking behind the door.

"I have him outside."

"Well, let him in."

That was all I could make out. I straightened

up and took my hands out of my pockets. Then the door opened.

Phil peeked his head out of the door. "Mr. Cragg will see you now."

I nodded and followed Phil through the door. I stepped into a large art room. The walls were covered with paintings and drawings from past classes. All of the tables were decorated with strokes of paint. It was a tall room, with windows near the ceiling. Craig sat in the very back, behind the art teacher's desk. I studied him as I crossed the room.

He was wearing a three-piece suit with a long, red tie. His hair was slicked back perfectly, like he was wearing a shiny, black helmet. He sat straight up in his chair with his hands locked together on top of the desk. When he opened his mouth to speak, the glare off a set of shiny white teeth hit me hard.

"Mr. Gummyshoes," Cragg said, "I have to say, it is against court regulations that I see you before the hearing."

"I won't take but a second of your time, Dan," I told him. "Can I call you Dan?"

"Mr. Cragg works best for me," he said, losing the smile.

"Well ... Mr. Cragg," I said. "I'll just cut to the chase. I want you to drop the case you have on Henry Gallagher."

Cragg laughed and said, "That will not happen, Mr. Gummyshoes."

"And why not?" I asked, losing my patience.

"Mr. Gummyshoes, I recognize and respect the fact that you are a professional," Cragg said. "Although I think sleuthing is hardly a profession, if you want to know my honest opinion. I can see that you, like myself, pride yourself on how you look professionally. If you take a case, then you make sure your client is satisfied with your work. Am I correct?"

"Yeah," I said sternly. "What of it?"

"Well unfortunately, too many fellow students have fallen victim to Mr. Gallagher's rather explosive science fair project." He let out a little laugh. "If I just drop the case like you ask of me, how will I look then?"

I didn't like the words coming out of his mouth, but he made sense.

"Being the professional that I am, Mr. Gummyshoes," he continued, "I have already done extensive research on the explosion. It wasn't caused by mixing baking soda and vinegar like everyone assumes." He sat back in his chair. "It was caused by soda pop that was poured into crushed up candy." He leaned forward. "I don't suppose I'm doing my job and yours now, am I? Were you aware of this, Mr. Gummyshoes?"

I stared at him. Then I shook my head. "No."

He continued, "If Mr. Gallagher is indeed innocent, then you have no cause to worry when you appear at the hearing tomorrow." Cragg stood up and buttoned his suit jacket. "But until that time, I'm afraid we cannot speak any further. Good day, Mr. Gummyshoes. Phil will see you out."

Phil came up from behind and grabbed me by the elbow. I shook him off and walked out of the art room on my own. I turned back around once more and opened my mouth to give Cragg a piece of my mind, but nothing came out. So I exited, letting him have the last word.

Walking back to Edwin West, I replayed the conversation over and over in my head. *There is no way I can be more convincing than that guy*, I thought. It made me nervous. I stopped 100 yards from the entrance of Edwin West. I could see there was a media frenzy led by Jeff Dawkins and his morning announcement crew. I couldn't hear what they are saying but I could only assume it was about the court hearing the next day. I ran around the campus to the back entrance of the school, avoiding all of the hoopla.

The clock on the wall read 12:58 p.m. I had just enough time to grab my books from my locker and get to class. I spun the combo on my lock and gave the door a firm yank. To my surprise, a folded up piece of paper fell to the floor. I looked around. Then I bent down and picked it up. After unfolding it, I saw a message written in neat handwriting with green ink. The message read:

If you want to crack the case, the answers are in the numbers. 4000/102186.

I looked around again to see if anyone was watching. Just then the second bell rang and I was officially late for class.

CHAPTER 6
Stolen Solution

Later that day, MacGuffin and I were video chatting. He was at his house while I was back at school in my office. I showed him the note with the numbers. He looked as confused as I felt.

"Maybe it's long division," he said looking at me past the paper.

"What do you mean?" I asked, while scratching Little Ricky behind the ear, just how he liked it. I had snuck him into my office to keep me company since no one else was supposed to be in school at that hour.

"Well, look at the slash between 4000 and

102186. That is usually the symbol for division," MacGuffin responded. He punched the numbers into a calculator on his desk.

I watched for a minute. "So what do we have?"

He looked over his work and scratched his head with his index finger. "Well, if you divide 4000 by 102186, the answer is .03914431. Does that have any relevance to you or the case?"

I stared at him dumbly. He noticed my face and started punching again. "If you add up 10, 21, and 86, you get 117. If you divide 4000 by 117, you get 34.1880342. Does that have any relevance to you or ..."

"Let's forget the math, Mac," I said. "Somebody out there is trying to mess with my mind, but I've got news for them. It's going to take a lot more than just a simple riddle of numbers to trip me up, pal."

Then I heard a ruckus outside my office doors. I peered through the window and saw hordes of students outside in the hall.

"Oh, for Pete's sake," I said, opening the door. Loud yells and camera flashes were popping off a million a second. I tried to shield my eyes with my hand.

"Mr. Gummyshoes, Mr. Gummyshoes," Jeff Dawkins said, holding the microphone up to his mouth, "is it true that you are totally unprepared for this upcoming case and that it's likely that Henry Gallagher will be found guilty?" Jeff shoved the microphone in my face.

I looked at Jeff and then into the camera. "Well, Jeff. I don't think anything is certain at this point in the case."

"Another question," Jeff interrupted. "If he is found guilty, are you fully prepared to have the punishment that Henry Gallagher will receive on your hands?" Jeff shoved the microphone back in my face.

"I ... uh...," I said, pushing the microphone away from my nose. "I have to go." I turned on my heels, got into my office, and slammed the door shut before I could be asked any more questions.

"What was that all about?" MacGuffin asked.

"I have a feeling this case is going to get a lot harder before it gets any easier, chum," I replied to the computer screen.

"Can you give me those numbers again? I have an idea on how to crack them," MacGuffin asked.

Just then I felt a chilled draft blow through

my office. I walked toward the back of the classroom and noticed that the window was wide open. I slammed it shut and walked back to my desk. Something was wrong—not everything was on the desk where it once had been. I went through the desk, looking for what really mattered.

"What is it, Jon?" MacGuffin asked.

"Somebody just stole the solution to my case," I told him in shock.

CHAPTER 7

Desperate Words

I went home in despair. *What would I do without the note?* I thought. I woke up the next morning knowing that it was the day of the trial. I had no evidence, no witnesses, no nothin'. I had no choice but to face the music.

Before I did the usual morning routine, I went into my mom's office and sat in front of her computer. I punched in a few keys and moved the mouse. Before I knew it, Uncle Nicky was staring at me with half-open eyes. He's a handsome fella, usually sporting a pinstripe suit and slicked-back hair. But right then he was sporting pajamas and a messy hairdo.

"Hey, Shamus," he said in a groggy tone. "Great to hear from you, pal!"

Uncle Nicky liked to call me Shamus. It's an old name for a detective.

"Uncle Nicky, I need some advice," I said, looking at him through the webcam. "Today I have to provide evidence in a case and it doesn't look very good."

"Well your work is excellent, Shamus," Uncle Nicky told me. "I'm sure you will do a great job."

"I know that, Uncle Nicky," I told him. "I'm just saying that I might be outnumbered here. I was hoping you would have some way of helping me out of this."

"Have you asked all the questions that needed to be asked?" Uncle Nicky questioned.

"Yeah, I've asked everything I could about the case," I responded. "It was all a bust."

Uncle Nicky searched his desk and pulled out a pen. He sat back in his chair and tapped the pen on his knee, like he usually did when he was thinking about what to say.

"Well, Shamus, my best advice is to do what you do best. And that's finding the true answers.

You are going to have to prove that you are the greatest detective the fourth grade has ever seen," he said. "If it's hard to prove, it'll be that much sweeter when you do your job right!"

He was right. It was easy for others to blame Hank—too easy. I had my work cut out for me, but I had to believe in my skills. It was up to me to find the real source of the problem. It would be hard, but hard is what I did best. I said good-bye to Uncle Nicky and logged off the computer.

I wasted no time getting to school. Maybe the stranger had left another note in my locker. I got to the entrance of Edwin West and went inside. The halls were empty.

I looked at the numbers on the lockers. They went all the way from 1 to 4000. Wait—4000? That was it! I ran down the halls watching the numbers jump: 350, 400, 450. I kept counting until I hit it—number 4000. It was Ben Christopher's locker. I stared at the lock and realized I didn't have the combination anymore. I grabbed the door and shook it as hard as I could. It wouldn't budge.

People started rolling through the school

entrance and I picked MacGuffin out of the crowd. "Mac! Mac! I figured it out!"

MacGuffin heard me and worked his way toward the locker.

"Ben Christopher's locker, Mac!" I said. "Number 4,000 is Ben Christopher's locker!"

"This is incredible!" MacGuffin said in excitement. "Well, open her up!"

"Well, we don't have the combo anymore. I was hoping you remembered it. Do you?" I asked.

"All I remember is 34.18 and 117," he said glumly.

My back hit the locker and I slid down to the floor. "The answers to my case are behind this locker and I have no way to see them." I thought for a second. "Unless...," I stood up. "Mac, where is Ben? I can just ask him for the combo."

"I haven't seen him," Mac responded. "Can't you just ask Principal Links to open it?"

"No, he won't do it," I answered. "There's something about privacy and school policy, whatever that means."

MacGuffin started shaking the locker door like I tried but it was no use. We weren't getting it open. I turned around and started walking. I should have been at Edwin East, anyways. Maybe I could find a clue there. As I walked, I noticed kids turning from their open lockers to watch me. I pushed the school door open, flooding my vision with sunlight and camera flashes.

"Mr. Gummyshoes, Mr. Gummyshoes, how are you feeling about the trial today? Do you think you will actually *help* Henry Gallagher?" Jeff asked, walking with me down the steps.

That was it. I turned back around to Jeff.

"You want to know how I feel, Jeff?" I shouted into the camera. "I'll tell you. Right now, I feel like all of you are about to get a dose of real detective work." Then I marched off to Edwin East.

Jeff looked into the camera and said, "Desperate words from a desperate guy. This is Jeff Dawkins, reporting live from the trial of the century."

CHAPTER 8
Word for Word

An hour later, we were all sitting in the art room at Edwin East. And by *we*, I mean most of the students from Edwin West and Edwin East. I sat next to Hank at a table facing the desk at the front of the room. I opened up my notebook and set it down on the table. The rest of the students sat behind us. The room was filled with voices, mostly whispers. I tried to think about how I was going to present my evidence. Mostly I thought about locker 4000.

Cragg walked into the art room and down the aisle past the rest of the students. He took a seat at the table to the left of mine. He placed his briefcase on top of the table, rolled the combination in, and snapped it open. He took out a thick pile of paper and folders and laid it neatly in front of him with a number of pens. When he was situated, he looked over at me and saw that I wasn't ready to go down without a fight. He gave me a smirk. Principal Links and Principal Ant walked into the art room and sat down behind the desk.

"We are all here because of a terrible incident that happened at Edwin West Elementary last week," Principal Ant said. "A science fair project went haywire and messed up the entire gymnasium and destroyed the surrounding projects. Today, we will hear from the accused, Henry Gallagher. We will decide on the punishment after all has been said."

I sat up in my chair and felt a bead of sweat roll down my cheek. "Gee, Jon," I heard Hank whisper into my ear, "I really hope you know what you're doing."

"Don't worry, chum. I have this under control," I whispered back without looking at him.

"Mr. Gallagher, you may take the podium," Principal Ant said.

I leaned back and got close to Hank's ear. "Just go up there and tell the truth. I have your back."

So Hank went to the podium and gave them his spiel. It was exactly how he laid it down for me, word for word.

"Thank you, Mr. Gallagher, please have a seat," Principal Links said.

Hank sat back down next to me and let out a loud and relieved sigh. I looked over at him, gave him a wink, and looked at the two principals.

"Mr. Cragg, you're up," Principal Ant ordered.

Cragg stood up and buttoned the top button of his coat. "Thank you, Principal Ant." He turned and faced the students sitting behind us. "Now, with my experience in the debate club, I've learned a few things. For one, every argument has two sides. One is correct, and the other is, simply put, wrong. Now, the tale Mr. Gallagher has told us was quite fascinating— but was it true? We had Frankie Flats taste the solution that came from the model volcano. It was determined it wasn't a mix of baking soda and vinegar, but that of crushed-up candy and soda pop."

"What are you getting at, Mr. Cragg?" Principal Ant asked from behind his desk.

"Principal Ant, Principal Links, if you will," Cragg said pointing at the classroom door, "I have one witness who I would like to question."

And just then, Ben Christopher walked through the door. He made his way to the front of the classroom and stood at the podium.

"Ambassador Christopher, how long have you known the accused, Mr. Gallagher?" Cragg asked.

"Well, since we were in kindergarten together. And every semester he runs against me in the student elections. So I get some face time with him," Ben responded coolly.

"And in this extensive face time you've had with Mr. Gallagher, could you tell that he was prone to this type of destruction or mischief?" Cragg asked.

"Absolutely," Ben responded. "He has always been a sore loser after the elections. He tears down all of my posters right after I put them up!"

The crowd behind us gave a loud gasp.

"That's a bold-faced lie!" Hank screamed as he leaped from his chair.

"Okay, okay, everyone relax," Principal Links said, raising his hands in the air. "We're going to take a 20-minute recess, so everyone can cool down. We will continue after."

Outside, I watched as everyone else enjoyed the recess while I held Little Ricky's leash.

"Thanks for grabbing Little Ricky for me, Mac. He usually cheers me up," I said, watching Little Ricky eat some dropped candy that was frozen in the snow.

"Maybe this is a sign, Mac. Maybe I'm just not cut out for the game," I continued.

"Don't say that, Jon," Mac said.

"No, it's true, Mac. Let people believe the easiest answers. That's fine with me. I'm through finding the hard answers," I said.

Just then, I heard Little Ricky cough. He sounded like an old man clearing his throat.

"Is he okay?" MacGuffin asked with a worried look on his face.

"Yeah, he's fine. He always yaks up whenever he eats too much garbage," I said watching Little

Ricky as he made his odd noises. "He does this at home all of the time."

"Have you guys seen my ants?" I heard an angelic voice ask from behind us. It was Amber Holiday. "You know, my science fair project? They're the ants that are different colors. I left my jar open and they escaped!"

"Sorry, Ms. Holiday. I haven't seen them. We've been watching Little Ricky this whole time," I replied back with a weak smile.

Little Ricky coughed again. This time garbage started to come out of his mouth.

"Ewww," Amber said stepping back from the puke.

First it was the red piece of candy he had just eaten out of the snow. The next things out were Amber's red, green, and orange ants, that quickly scurried away. The last thing was a crumpled up piece of paper. Wait, paper? *No! It couldn't be!*

I bent down and picked up the steaming, slimy piece of paper. I unfolded it and saw:

4000/102186

"Mac, we've got to go to Edwin West," I said with the biggest smile that my face had ever made. I picked Little Ricky up off the ground, pointed his face toward mine, and planted a big kiss on him.

"But we're due back in court in 20 minutes! There's no way we can get there and back in time," he said.

"Not unless we stall the court," I told him.

"And how are we going to do that?" MacGuffin asked.

I looked around the jungle gym and found my guy. I whistled and watched him run to us.

"Phil, you said you work little jobs here and there, right?" I said to the boy in the full snowsuit and ski mask.

"For a price, yeah," he replied.

I dug in my pocket and pulled out a pack of gum. Phil stared at it. "How about you entertain a courtroom for a couple minutes."

He looked at the pack of gum, grabbed it out of my hand, and gave me a nod.

I looked over to MacGuffin, "Shall we?"

We made it to Edwin West in record time. MacGuffin and I ran down the halls until we finally hit number 4000. I did not waste a second. I spun in the combination, pushed the tab up, and yanked the door open. MacGuffin stumbled back in shock, but I just smiled.

"Bingo," I said.

CHAPTER 9
The Combination

MacGuffin and I got to the art room door ten minutes after recess had ended. We stopped to make ourselves presentable.

"How do I look?" I asked MacGuffin.

"Like a detective," MacGuffin responded.

"Well," I said, fixing my collar, "there's no time like showtime." And like that, we were through the door.

Phil was standing in front of everyone doing some sort of stand-up routine. "And so he says, 'But, officer, it's the same dog!'" The punch line made the whole room chuckle.

"That will be quite enough, Phil. I'll take it from here," I said.

"Mr. Gummyshoes, where have you been? We've been waiting for you at the request of Mr. Gallagher," Principal Ant barked from behind the desk.

I put my hand up. "I have a few words, if you don't mind."

Principal Ant thought for a second and said, "Proceed," he said.

"Thank you." I turned toward the rest of the room. "Ladies and gentlemen, I stand before you with a person you assume is guilty. You may even be ready to give him a punishment. But like Mr. Cragg has mentioned, there are always two sides to an argument."

Principal Ant sat back in his chair. "Spare us the theatrics, Gummyshoes, and just tell us what you have."

I straightened up. "Right, well, this case may look simple, but it goes a lot deeper than the trouble caused at the science fair." I stepped around the desk and walked in front of the crowd. "This plunges us into the politics of our school and how one is perceived through popularity."

"I'm losing my patience," Principal Ant said, checking his watch.

"I have evidence proving that Ben Christopher was the mastermind behind the destruction of this year's science fair," I said.

The entire room gasped. Ben rose to his feet.

"This is absolutely ridiculous!" Ben screamed.

"All right, all right, everyone calm down!" Principal Ant shouted.

"Gummyshoes, these are some serious allegations you're throwing out here," Principal Links said. "Do you have any evidence to prove this?"

I crossed my arms and leaned up against the desk. "Do I have evidence? Why, if you'll follow me to Edwin West, I'll show you all the evidence you need, Chief."

We all headed over to Edwin West. We marched down the halls to locker 4000 and stopped.

I looked at Ben. "Is this your locker, Mr. Christopher?"

"You know it is, Gummyshoes. What about it?" Ben snarled.

"Will you please open it up using your combination?" I asked, crossing my arms.

Ben looked at me and then at the principals. He let out a sigh and then started twisting the combination. He pulled the locker door open and the rest was history.

"Wait. I don't know what any of this stuff is," Ben said, stumbling back.

In his locker was a big bag of candy, bottles of soda pop, and a book on how to build model volcanoes—all the ingredients needed to build one extremely explosive science fair project.

"But ... but ... this stuff isn't mine!" Ben pleaded. "I'm never at my locker because I'm on the streets trying to win my campaign!"

"And here lies the motive." I said. "You couldn't handle the pressure of having someone run against you. You wanted to keep it as easy as possible. Like you said, Principal Links was going to personally endorse you to win. With Hank out of the picture, you would never have to worry about winning again!"

"But, I don't even like candy!" Ben cried. "I haven't had to go to the dentist in years because of how well I keep my teeth!'

I looked over to Principal Links. "Chief, I request that you drop all charges on Henry Gallagher for the crime of destroying the school gym. At least until further investigation can be done."

"I think you're right, Gummyshoes." Principal Links put his hand on Ben's shoulder. "Let's go, Ben. We're going to have to call your folks."

Principal Links took Ben and I was left with the crowd. Then I saw Amber and pushed my way toward her.

"I'm sorry about Little Ricky eating your project, Ms. Holiday," I said. "He can be a bit much sometimes."

"It's okay, Jon. I can understand why he would want to lick them up. I shouldn't have made them look so much like candy," she replied.

I let out a chuckle, "I'll say."

Then I stopped laughing and thought about what she said: *candy*. I looked through my notebook and found what I was looking for. It seemed like there was one more stop for me to make that day.

CHAPTER 10

The Hard Answers

Later that day, I went back to my office. I sat forward in my chair, just so I could get a better look at Hank as he walked into the room.

Hank stopped in front of my desk and put his hands out. "You did it. You really did it! You believed in me and made what was once wrong right. I cannot thank you enough, Jon."

"Sure, Hank. All in a day's work, I guess," I told him.

"Well, I better be off. Mom is taking me out for a celebratory dinner," he said excitedly. "And I'm going to start thinking about running in the election this year! I figure, since Ben is out of the running, I'll have a real chance of actually making it!"

I blew some air out and looked away. "Swell."

"Thanks again, pal." Hank turned on his heel and started making his way toward the door.

"I stopped by your dentist's office today," I said, watching those words stop Hank dead in his tracks.

"Oh, yeah?" He asked without turning toward me. "And why would you do that?"

"Oh, you know, just a hunch. I figured I hadn't really gotten all of the answers I needed for the case," I said.

He turned around. "And what did he say?"

"He said you had quite a few questions for him," I said, looking at some dirt that was under my nail. Then I looked up at him and his red face. "Specifically about the reaction between candy and soda pop. You know, those two things you had to quit on account of the cavities."

He found a seat in front of my desk and smiled. "Well, look at you. Finally going after the real, hard answers."

I flicked the dirt from my nail and looked up at the real criminal. "Let me lay it out for you, Hank. You're a forgettable guy, from what I gather. Your own mother doesn't even know your name. So you made a plan that would get you seen by all. Your name would be recognized. You sabotaged your own science fair project and made a mess that was big enough to even get Links's attention. You'd have to be innocent somehow, so you planted all of the materials in Ben's locker. You're his locker neighbor, so you scoped his combination and schedule."

I took a breath.

"Knowing that I was good at what I do, you came to me with everything set up for me to find. The note with the combination written on it with that green pen," I pointed up to the green pen sticking out of his shirt pocket, "and the materials for the exploding volcano." I sat back in my chair. "You were out to make a name for yourself, eliminate Ben, and finally win the school election. And you used me to try to get it."

Hank's smile widened. "You really are great at what you do, Jon. I won't lie. You got everything."

He clapped his hands and stood up. "But the thing is, it's over. There is no stopping me now. My genius plan has made me a celebrity and Ben has been expelled from Edwin West. I will finally have my shot at this election and everyone will remember me." He lost his smile. "It's a shame it had to end this way. But I must be going."

"I agree that it is a shame it had to end this way," I said, turning the computer around to face Hank. Principal Links's face was on the screen. "You got that?" I asked him.

"Sure did," Links responded. "Henry, can I see you in my office for a minute?"

Hank's smile quickly faded.

"Like I said, Hank. Some kids win the science fair. Others? They go to state in soccer." I stood up and straightened my shirt. "Me? I solve mysteries."

Hank left without another word. As I was putting my coat on, MacGuffin arrived to hear the news. Soon the whole school found out. The media went crazy after they heard that Hank was really behind everything and that Ben would be back in office. MacGuffin and I waited for the commotion to die down.

Out in the hallway, Becky Lipgloss approached us.

"Hi, Larry," she said.

"Well, hey, Becky," MacGuffin said back.

"Did you really help Jon win that case against Henry Gallagher?" she asked.

MacGuffin stumbled over his words for a second, so I piped in. "Of course he did, Ms. Lipgloss. In fact, if it weren't for his master detective skills, I wouldn't have gotten out of that jam unless I was spread on toast."

Becky looked from me to Mac excitedly and asked, "Really?!"

MacGuffin didn't say anything, but he nodded frantically.

"Say, Larry, I was wondering. Do you want to walk me to Ice Man's for a quick cone?" Becky asked.

MacGuffin didn't stop nodding. They walked off together, leaving me alone once again. So I headed toward the exit. I opened the door and was flooded with camera flashes yet again. Snow had begun to dance around the sky once more.

"Mr. Gummyshoes, Mr. Gummyshoes! You've not only proven yourself as a true detective

among many fakes, but you've foiled what could possibly have been the biggest scam in any school district in this county," Jeff Dawkins exclaimed, shoving the camera into my face. "What's next for you?"

That was a good question. I scanned the crowd. And then I saw Amber in the back staring at me with a smile. I looked Jeff in the eyes and let him have it.

"Well, Jeff," I told him, " I was thinking about getting into politics."

X Hank's gloves were moved when he came back from the water fountain.

X Cragg says the explosion was caused by soda pop and crushed candy.

X Mysterious note in my locker. Who wrote it???

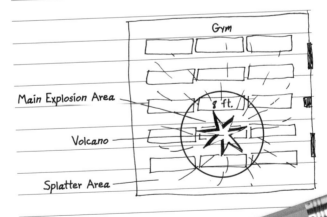

Gym

Main Explosion Area

8 ft.

Volcano

Splatter Area